GOOD WOOD BEAR

BIJOU LE TORD

BRADBURY PRESS · NEW YORK

Text and illustrations Copyright © 1985 by Bijou Le Tord.
All rights reserved. No part of this book may be reproduced or
transmitted in any form or by any means, electronic or mechanical,
including photocopying, recording or by any information storage
and retrieval system, without permission in writing from the Publisher.
Bradbury Press
An Affiliate of Macmillan, Inc.
866 Third Avenue, New York, N.Y. 10022
Collier Macmillan Canada, Inc.
Manufactured in the United States of America
10 9 8 7 6 5 4 3 2 1
The text of this book is set in 14 pt. Goudy Old Style.
The illustrations are black line drawings with full-color backgrounds.
Library of Congress Cataloging in Publication Data
Le Tord, Bijou.
Good wood bear.
Summary: With the assistance of Goose, Bear builds
a birdhouse so birds may live safely.
1. Children's stories, American. [1. Birdhouses—
Fiction. 2. Bears—Fiction. 3. Geese—Fiction]
I. Title.
PZ7.L568Go   1985   [E]   85-70864
ISBN 0-02-756440-1

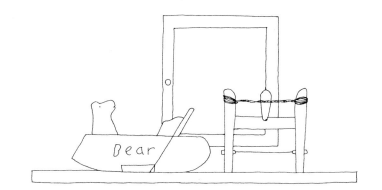

TO YANN

Early one morning
on my way to meet Bear
I found a bird's nest

with tiny spotted eggs.

I carried it to show Bear.

"Look Goose," said Bear,
"birds collect twigs
to weave their nests."

Bear decided to build
a small house for
birds to shelter in.

I watched him draw
plans and measure its
length, its width,
its height.

He chose fine wood
for each part
of his house.

With a sharp saw
he cut out the front,
and the back.

And guided his tool
down the sides,
and over the roof.

He made a window
shaped like
a heart.

Bear drilled holes
for thin wood pegs.

We listened to
the sound of his plane
gliding over the wood,
shoof, shoof.

He added tiny pegs
for birds to perch on

and made sure that
each part fit exactly.

He hammered silvery nails

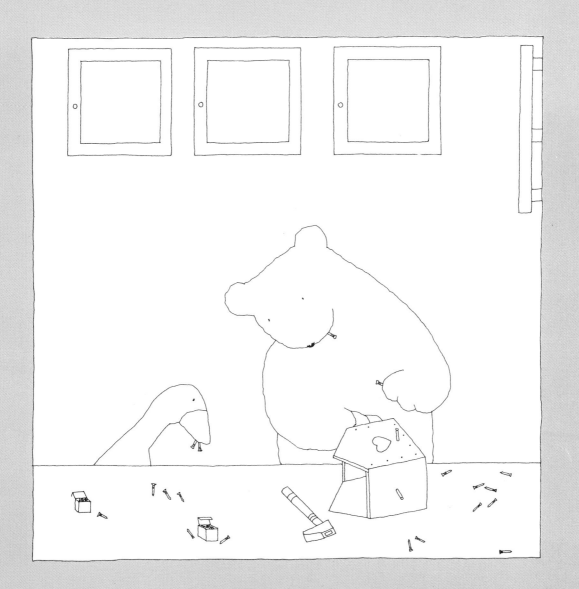

to hold together the sides,
the front, the back
and the bottom
of his birdhouse.

He nailed down the roof

and sanded it carefully.

Then he painted
the roof white,
a red trim, and
blue pegs.

While his house dried,
Bear whistled
the song of a finch,
tpik, tpik, tpik.

He put together
a wood pole and
a small board

for the house to sit on.

Outside he dug a deep hole

for his house
to stay firmly
in the ground.

We watched
chickadees
hop and flitter

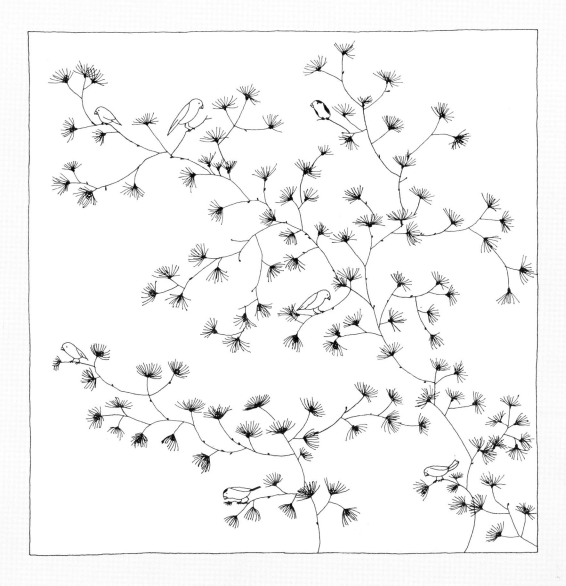

sparrows and finches
tweet and pick at
their new house.

Just before I left ⸻

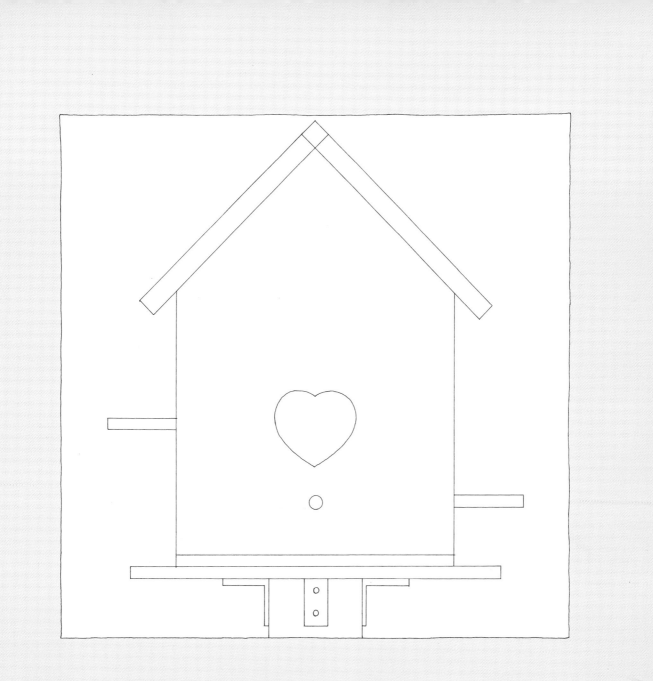

Bear gave me a drawing
of his birdhouse

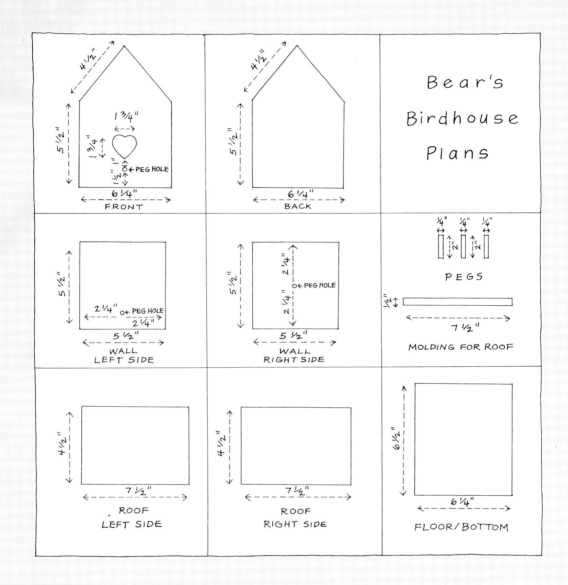

and plans to build
a house of my own.